THE AMAZING ADVENTURES OF THE DC SUPER-PETS!

The Battle of the Bots

by Steve Korté

illustrated by Mike Kunkel

PICTURE WINDOW BOOKS
a capstone imprint

Published by Picture Window Books, an imprint of Capstone.
1710 Roe Crest Drive
North Mankato, Minnesota 56003
capstonepub.com

Library of Congress Cataloging-in-Publication Data
Names: Korté, Steven, author. | Kunkel, Mike, 1969– illustrator.
Title: The battle of the bots / by Steve Korté ; illustrated by Mike Kunkel.
Description: North Mankato, Minnesota : Picture Window Books, [2022] |
Series: The amazing adventures of the DC super-pets | Audience: Ages 5–7
| Audience: Grades K–1 | Summary: Inside the giant robot he has built, Lex
Luthor is rampaging through Metropolis smashing buildings, and it is up
to Super Hero Cyborg, and his two pet robots, F.E.L.I.X. and M.A.X., to stop
Luthor and his mechanical monster.
Identifiers: LCCN 2021054379 (print) | LCCN 2021054380 (ebook) |
ISBN 9781666344479 (hardcover) | ISBN 9781666344516 (paperback) |
ISBN 9781666344523 (pdf)
Subjects: LCSH: Cyborg (Fictitious character)—Juvenile fiction. | Superheroes—
Juvenile fiction. | Supervillains—Juvenile fiction. | Robots—Juvenile fiction.
| CYAC: Superheroes—Fiction. | Supervillains—Fiction. | Robots—Fiction. |
LCGFT: Animal fiction.
Classification: LCC PZ7.K8385 Bat 2022 (print) | LCC PZ7.K8385 (ebook) |
DDC [E]—dc23
LC record available at https://lccn.loc.gov/2021054379
LC ebook record available at https://lccn.loc.gov/2021054380

Designed by Kay Fraser
Design Elements by Shutterstock/SilverCircle

TABLE OF CONTENTS

They are super-strong.

They are powerful and intelligent computers.

They are Cyborg's loyal companions.

These are . . .

THE AMAZING ADVENTURES OF

F.E.L.I.X. and M.A.X.

CHAPTER 1

Mechanical Monster

Far below the LexCorp building in Metropolis, the evil scientist Lex Luthor is hard at work. He is building a giant robot in his top-secret laboratory.

"My XL-LexBot is so big that no one will be able to defeat it!" says Lex. Then he climbs into the head of the robot.

Lex takes control of the massive machine. He steers the XL-LexBot onto the street.

CRASH!

The XL-LexBot shatters a brick

building with its arm!

SMASH!

The robot crushes an empty car

beneath its giant foot!

KER-BLAM!

The XL-LexBot smashes into a bank
and rips open its vault. Lex guides the
robot's arm to grab stacks of money.

RRRRRRING!

The bank's alarm fills the air.

"Good luck to any Super Heroes who
try to stop me!" Lex says with a chuckle.

The half human and half robot Super Hero Cyborg has heard the alarm. He flies toward the bank with his two pet robots F.E.L.I.X. and M.A.X. Cyborg built the bots years ago. They are very strong and intelligent.

CHAPTER 2

Robot Rampage

Cyborg and the bots arrive at the bank. The hero changes his right arm into a sonic cannon.

BOOM!

Sonic energy rays blast from Cyborg's

arm cannon. The rays bounce off the

XL-LexBot's thick armor.

ZING!

The sonic rays fly back toward Cyborg
and the two bots. The hero leans down
to protect F.E.L.I.X. and M.A.X.

"Cyborg, look out!" yells F.E.L.I.X.

The energy rays hit the back of Cyborg's head. It is one of the few spots where Cyborg is not protected by armor. Cyborg is knocked out.

Lex guides the XL-LexBot to grab the
sleeping Cyborg. The giant robot tosses
Cyborg out of the bank.

Cyborg lands in the middle of a
railroad track.

CHAPTER 3

Bots to the Rescue

"Come on, F.E.L.I.X. It's time to crush this big bad bot!" says M.A.X.

The two pet robots roll toward the XL-LexBot and crash into it.

WHAM!

But the tiny bots are too small to damage the giant robot.

Suddenly, a wave of flames shoots out of the XL-LexBot's hand. M.A.X. quickly presses a button on his chest. A metal shield pops out and covers the two tiny robots.

Lex laughs in triumph as he turns

the XL-LexBot and leaves the bank.

"I have a plan," says F.E.L.I.X.

The little bot grabs M.A.X. with one

of his hands. Then F.E.L.I.X. places his

other hand on the ground and pushes

up with all his strength.

F.E.L.I.X. and M.A.X. fly through the air and land on top of the XL-LexBot. The two tiny bots smash open the cockpit where Luthor is controlling his massive machine.

M.A.X. stretches his arms and
rips out the wires in the XL-LexBot's
control panel.

A cable shoots out of F.E.L.I.X. and
wraps around Luthor. The XL-LexBot
crashes to the ground.

F.E.L.I.X. and M.A.X. rush to the railroad track where Cyborg is sleeping.

TOOT! TOOT!

A train is racing down the track. The train's driver doesn't see Cyborg.

"I have an idea," says M.A.X. as he hops on top of F.E.L.I.X.

M.A.X. shines a powerful red light on the top of his antenna.

The train's driver thinks that the red light is a stoplight.

She pulls the brake seconds before the train can crash into Cyborg.

Minutes later, Cyborg sits up and rubs the back of his head. He is amazed to see the XL-LexBot on the ground and Lex Luthor tied up.

Cyborg hugs his two super-intelligent robot pets.

"You two have been busy," says Cyborg with a smile. "I should have known that giant robot would be no match for my two brainy bots!"

AUTHOR!

Steve Korté is the author of many books for children and young adults. He worked for many years at DC Comics, where he edited more than 600 books about Superman, Batman, Wonder Woman, and the other heroes and villains in the DC Universe. He lives in New York City with his husband, Bill, and their super-cat, Duke.

ILLUSTRATOR!

Mike Kunkel wanted to be a cartoonist ever since he was a little kid. He has worked on numerous projects in animation and books, including many years spent drawing cartoon stories about creatures and super heroes such as the Smurfs and Shazam. He has won the Annie Award for Best Character Design in an Animated Television Production and is the creator of the two-time Eisner Award-winning comic book series Herobear and the Kid. Mike lives in southern California, and he spends most of his extra time drawing cartoons filled with puns, trying to learn new magic tricks, and playing games with his family.

"Word Power"

armor (AR-muhr)—a protective metal covering

cockpit (KOK-pit)—the place where the driver of a giant robot sits

defeat (di-FEET)—to beat someone in a competition

intelligent (in-TEL-uh-jent)—very smart

laboratory (LAB-bruh-tor-ee)—a place where scientists do experiments, tests, and investigations

massive (MASS-iv)—very large

protect (proh-TEKT)—to guard or keep safe from harm

shield (SHEELD)—an object that gives protection from harm

sonic (SON-ik)—having to do with sound waves

vault (VAWLT)—a safe room to store things of value

WRITING PROMPTS

1. F.E.L.I.X. is short for Fantastically Excellent Logistically Intelligent X-Treme. M.A.X. is short for Magnificently Artificially X-Treme. Write your name out in letters like theirs. Then write down a word that each letter stands for.

2. If you could design a giant robot, what would it look like? Write a paragraph describing your robot. Then draw a picture of it.

3. At the end of the story, Lex Luthor and his giant robot have been captured. Write a new chapter that describes what happens to the villain and his robot next. You decide!

DISCUSSION QUESTIONS

1. F.E.L.I.X. and M.A.X. work together to save Cyborg. What makes them such good teammates?

2. Lex Luthor uses his giant robot to commit crimes. How might a giant robot like Luthor's be used for good?

3. If you could build a robot, would you make it huge like Lex Luthor's or small like Cyborg's? Explain your answer.

THE AMAZING ADVENTURES OF THE DC SUPER-PETS!

Collect them all!